Introduction

This long poem is my way of sharing the history and atmosphere of the Fens where I lived for twenty years. For five of those years I wrote monthly articles for *The Cambridgeshire Journal* about the history of the county. Many of these were about the Black Fens.

In 2001 a partnership of Natural England, the Environment Agency, the Wild Life Trust, Huntingdonshire District Council and the Middle Level Drainage Commissioners was set up to begin work on **The Great Fen Project**. This is a long term plan to create 3,700 hectares of wetland between Huntingdon and Peterborough to connect two existing Nature Reserves, Woodwalton Fen and Holme Fen. These reserves are the final remnants of the great East Anglian wetland drained in the mid nineteenth century. The land will be a haven for the special flora and fauna of the area and a green space for people.

The poem moves backwards and forwards in time as it creates the elemental aspect of the area and shows it in its different moods.

C.R.

Black Fen

An East wind whistles from
North Sea to low land,
hisses and wails
around house walls,
yells on corners,
rattles down pipes,
bangs dustbin lids,
bursts into dreams,
turns them to nightmares.

Houses reveal themselves in a land of horizontals.

Our house sank in one corner after floods
of sixty years ago or more. Now it tips visitors
towards out of kilter windows,
from which are views of too much sky.
Outside is a landscape where single trees
are blown to forty five degrees. Outbuildings lean,
corrugated iron buckles, land sinks year by year.

▪ ▪ ▪

Long ago this was a world of wych elm, lindens, oak.
Primaeval forest that grew to a hundred feet or more,
branchless trunks, topped by crowns of leaves.
Floods felled trees, another forest grew where Neolithic
hunters chased wild boar, leaving flint arrow heads.

Floods returned. The next forest was willow, alder, pine, birch,
layer on layer of trees, tree trunks buried but not decayed,
waiting.

Bulldozers prize up bog oak, aeons old.
Monstrous trunks harden in the air,
split, reveal inner layers,
become rock-like, unusable. Their fate
to be sacrificially returned to the elements,
burnt with an acrid reek of marsh and fen.

Landgirls stand, deep in fen soil
blackened by its darkness.
They and their farmer agree. Dig for Victory—'yes'.
Dig up one ninety foot long bog oak.
'No'. Dynamite is the answer
Everything else is being blown up,
why not this bit of wood as well?

Sticks of dynamite are laid, fuses run and lit,
The wood fossil explodes, pieces turn high in the air,
splinters soar, log-size sections tumble and roll.
Ancient wood becomes fractured fragments.

Bog oak has other uses
fences, garden furniture, sometimes
sculpture.

Carrion crow, crooked and harsh,
carved from cracked bog oak,
hard as granite. Fossilised wood
that must be gouged with power tools,
burnt, scraped to shape it anew;
transformed into animals or religious figures,
Christ, gaping wood gashes for wounds,
Mary, splitting with tears.

A pile of ancient pine roots stands by the road side.
People disentangle speciments for future use.
The rest is burned, a funeral pyre.
History gone up in smoke.

▪ ▪ ▪

Morning mist hovers over Fens
disguising shapes.
It is seven hundred A.D.
South of the Wash, below the siltlands, lie the Fens.
Low-lying, windswept, water retaining as rivers
silt up. The Ouse, Nene, Welland,
meander across this peat plain. Shallow lakes
link across the centre. Water lies over the land
in winter, summer, cattle graze.
Sedges, reeds, wildfowl and fishes are its riches.
Only bird song and wind howl break the silence;
vast, flat space, three-quarters sky.

Then the monks come.

Throughout the Fens religious communities were formed on clay islands, Ramsey, Thorney, Crowland, Ely.

“We row into a whispering wind, along winding rivers
to seek an island we can settle. Man can find God
in such isolation. Only the movement of fish, writhing of eels
rippling of reed-heads accompany our slow journey.
When we find this place, we will create a community,
build a wooden church, pray in thankfulness.

Our lives are dedicated to God, isolated, on this island
surrounded by a sea of waving reeds, an unquiet,
desolate place, full of fish, fowl, eels to fill our bellies
and the King’s. He orders ten dozen wild fowl
for a feast, swans for a banquet. Orchards, vegetable
gardens flourish within our walls.

We give thanks to God.

Vows of Poverty, Obedience, Chastity bind us. In Eight
Sacred Offices we kneel to God from before sunrise
into the evening, such is the cycle of our devotions.
Tasks of living bend us in labour. We sow, plough,
tend our gardens, teach, minister to the sick.
We have our own ways to serve.

We give thanks to God.

Our relics, a piece of the cross, a saint's knuckle bone,
draw pilgrims to us over summer pathways.
Stories of a world beyond come with them,
tales of troubles, pestilence and war. We listen,
protect our treasures, tend our lands that stretch
far out across the Fens. We remain a still, calm place.

Thanks be to God."

The monasteries survive attacks by the Vikings, fires and plague, but with the Dissolution of 1539 King Henry the Eighth managed what all previous disasters could not do, destroy the religious houses of England and Wales. In 1536 there were over eight hundred monasteries, nunneries and priories. By 1540 there were none. Some Bishoprics, such as Ely and Peterborough became cathedrals.

Each carefully cut stone, once so laboured over,
mason's marks still visible,
disassembled.
Stone by stone the Abbeys are destroyed.
The King sells what he has claimed.
Land and buildings become the property
of rich landowners.
Loaded onto carts or boats, this crafted Barnak limestone
is conveyed to Cambridge to build new colleges,
Cauis, Kings, Trinity;
carted to Huntingdon for Hinchingbroke House,
carried away to form a different world.

▪ ▪ ▪

Not just a wind, wind we are used to.
Living in the flat lands
you are exposed.
This is different,
it blows in from everywhere
Friends may have seen it coming,
tried to advise. Told us to duck down,
or get away. But it comes,
slams into life,
crashes the exits shut,
tosses our lives in the air.

By Ugg Mere, John steps from dry mound
to rye tussock over skeins of dark water.
The twelve year old is hunter gatherer, egg collector.

A tufted duck rises from across a broad rivulet,
its eggs and nest tucked into tall grass.

John jumps onto an oozing mud bank,
slides backwards, lurches forward,
grasps at grass, scrabbles to find a toe hold.

Water laps at his feet as he thrashes
like an eel in a net. Shouts, he shouts
out across the mere to be answered
by a grebe's descending trill.

Water engulfs his heart, covers his shoulders;
Ripples run over his head, separate his hair
into tendrils of water weed.

▪ ▪ ▪

A stubble field, defined by ditches,
from the end bank the cottage seems
an horizon squatting doll's house.
This long, narrow strip will be a garden.
Our farmer neighbour sows meadow grass.
It rains and a green sward provides
the base colour for the garden canvas.
A vegetable plot is dug near the house,
rich, stoneless blue-black earth, 'Harrod's soil'
a friend quips. Then an orchard, surrounded
by native hedging, planted in a gale.
Ponds dug for water lilies, dragon flies,
finally trees, willows, beeches, birches
and a lilac hedge for butterflies.
At the very end are three poplars,
an oak bench, sculpture to sit on,
meditate, watch the sun, follow its progress
from rising to setting, feel the wind.
Hardly a day without soft breeze or gale,
so severe sometimes
I battle back to the house,
or crawl.

▪ ▪ ▪

Whittlesey Mere

Two thousand acres of sky
reflected in a shallow, fresh water lake,
teeming with clattering geese, coots,
dabchicks, mallard, tufted ducks with chicks in tow.
Herons, stiff extensions of dead trees,
bend branch-like necks towards the water
to see perch, large pike, burbots, lampreys.
Men wait in boats, gun at the prow pointing,
ready to dispatch thirty duck a blast.

Sails sing in an encountered wind
as myriad craft tack across the mere
in summer sailing races.
Reflected triangles fracture in ripples.
Spectators cheer.

Rivers rise and rise with winter rains, banks leak, burst.
Water flows out across fen fields, forming one vast lake,
inches deep. Frost transforms it into green glass-like ice,
perfect skating rink. First arrivals, local families,
their patterns sharpened, curved blades screwed
into ordinary working boots, straps softened or replaced.
They are ready. Soon straight lines and perfect circles
are cut into ice by the confident, meanderings by the uncertain,
criss-cross crazy lines at the edge - children and beginners.
Around the rink old men gather, skating days over.

A run of cold days; word has spread, crowds come
in carriages, on bicycles, along frozen rivers and drains.
A shot-like crack scatters everyone to the sides for safety
and the old men laugh, nudge each other and point
to a dark zig-zag line. The ice has snapped
under the weight of numbers but there are no drownings
only drama. Time for skating competitions on fields,
rivers, meres, drains. Men lean forward, arms swinging,
skimming to victory but no man can beat those brothers,
Turkey and Fish Carter, champions of the Fens.

Driving back from Peterborough I see
Brueghel-like figures skate
in multi-coloured scarves,
on azure ice against a winter sun;
recreating, if only for a day,
the pictures of last century
prior to climate change.
This winter scene is on frozen water
by a great sluice gate.
The skating competition,
impromptu product of minus zero,
is advertised for the next day.
It rains. Competition cancelled.

▪ ▪ ▪

Mists settle, all is pearl-grey,
de-focused. Reed stalks rattle, reed heads whisper
secrets of a low land, water drenched.

Fly high over the Fens now and see
straight lines, geometry of square, rectangle.
Lines take water where it ought to go,
out to the sea, fast.
Straight lines are drainage ditches,
dykes, rivers.

"Drain it, dig it, sew, harvest, reap profits."
Adventurer's talk, seventeenth century entrepreneurs
invest to impose their names on the landscape.

'Adventurer's Fens' all over the map. The Earl of Bedford
has his rivers, old and new; the river Ouse
straight jacketed into two parallel lines out to the Wash.

Vermuyden, a Dutchman and a drainage specialist, was hired by the Adventurers in 1634 to drain the land. He left Dagenham and The Thames Marshes to come to the Fens.

Straightness is dug into the landscape,
sluices control tide and water flow.
River water races to the sea.

For wildfowlers, fishermen, eelers, reedcutters
water is their world, not drained land.
They burn sluices, block ditches,
brake open river banks, let water return.
But to no avail,
the Adventurers prevail,
the land dries.

Soil, sponge-like, water holding,
once dried becomes light
decomposes, blows away.

This is a Fen Blow.
It whips in low, underhand, underfoot,
cuts a straight course at knee level,
loosens crops, plucks sugar beet
turns them in the air, flings them elsewhere.

This wind gets to work, rips in, reaches
right down to ground level, lifts dark soil,
browns the light; a fog of earth.
A wind of dust infiltrates,
insinuates.

One crack and it coats, clogs.
We should have known,
covered up. But we did not know,
we never do. There's always a crack,
somewhere.

■ ■ ■

Floods return
as ploughed land sinks below river beds.
Water knows its old lying place, lays low,
remains still. Man requires movement.
Across the Fens windpump sails turn,
a land of windmills, a world to tilt at.
Overtime even windpumps cannot cope.
Floods return.

Builders take up our kitchen floor.
Since the house leant everything is angled,
working surfaces send round objects rolling,
eggs smash, even crockery will slide and crash.

Damp seeps up through concrete,
This is still wetland, dykes either side,
flood marks from the Old River Nene
painted high on the outside wall.

Now dryness is required by Building Regs.
The kitchen floor opens up, reveals
flat, cream-coloured bricks laid on earth,
used in old Fen houses.

Last century, water would flood between the bricks,
with furniture chocked up, single storey house dwellers
walked the plank to bed. Water seeping away would
cause the soil to sink and heave, leave bricks uneven

needing to be re-laid each year. Our bricks are up
replaced with damp-proofed, level conrete.
I hold one cream brick in my hand and wonder
how to use it usefully.

Over time even wind and sail fail.
Only steam has the power to shift
water up and away. Steam
driving beam engines,
driving river waters seawards.

Steam can shift two thousand acres of water.
Time for Whittlesey Mere to disappear.
Time to sink a cast iron post through peat into clay,
top level with the soil, an eighteen fifty one experiment.
Water flows away into rivers and ditches.
Leaving a crustacean white surface on which
are found the censor and incense boat from Ramsey Abbey.
How they came there known only to the monks.

At Holme Fen Wood two posts stand.
The cast iron one appears to have risen up
from the earth, held in place by wires.
In reality the peat has sunk away,
its progress marked on the companion post.
This is one of the lowest places in England,
jump and the land quivers.

On the edge of rich farm land, by the cast iron post,
birch and alder are planted for a pheasant covet.
Remains of mere-side land, acid grassland,
heath and raised bog,
now a Nature Reserve.

Massed verticals in a horizontal landscape,
are a haven from this all-sky world.
Inside ditches divide and alder grow,
offer a tunnel view of winding paths, white birches
dark slashes in their bright bark,
angled roots of ripped up trees
blown over in a fen gale, trunks broken.
At the centre
a charcoal burner's kiln, redolent of hot metal,
wood smoke lingering, voices.

Now, woodpeckers hammer,
muntjack bark, walkers call their dogs.
Swans fly in feet forward onto newly dug lake.
Pine and oak grow amongst the birch,
perfumed honeysuckle drapes over bushes,
bracken and heather spread.
Along paths foxgloves cluster
cream, white, purple, pink,
darker marks in their delicate bells.
Shafts of light play on emerald moss,
a world, never wild but left alone.

▪ ▪ ▪

Fen deichers, digging dykes for the Dutchmen
become, through dialect twists perhaps,
Fen Tigers, working the drained land. Peat land
fuel gives men employment,
back breaking work, peat digging, down in Jackson's Fen.

To turn three thousand turf a day brings blisters,
cracked skin and pain in the wet ditch.
After years of digging, men like Old Henry
curve over to face the earth, walking with sticks
more quadrupeds than men.

Sam, the turf digger, sees an adder,
plenty of them in this wild place, teases it
with his bright spade. Hit with venom, the metal
colours brilliant blue-green. Sam laughs,
wipes his forehead with a cloth, ties it to a pole
and sets it into the soil a few yards away.
A cloud of mosquitos gather around the cloth,
leave Sam alone at his work.

Precise, measured work it is.
Each cess, or turf, six and a half by four and a half,
by three quarter inches. Land cleared,
pared, stumped out, lines set for digging.
One line dug, sixteen cesses set off the spade
onto the 'staddle', cleared land nearbye.
The piled turf is three blocks high, 'walls',
at the bottom, 'eccles' on top.

Old men past digging, dress
and dry the peat in complex patterns
so every cess is aired. They edge,
raise, turn and raffle them.
Three months for drying, then time to move
the blocks to the river side, ricked
into turf barrows, of one hundred
and twenty cesses, carefully wedged.

To load a barge, men run their piled turf barrows
from the high river bank fast,
fast down a narrow plank
so as not to fall.

▪ ▪ ▪

In these fens you could stand on earth
and not know it burns beneath
your feet. A match, a piece of glass
and grass will flare, flames go up,
flames go down, pit into peat.
Spirals, spurs of smoke seep up,
indicators of fire ready to blaze.
A spark from a steam engine sets a fen
aflame; it smoulders for two years.

From our window I see a bonfire
lit by farm workers down by the river.
It smokes for days, a week, a month.
At last men come to dig it out,
a vast scorched hole of burnt peat.

▪ ▪ ▪

Mud dries on droves as summer comes,
dyke water is low but yellow irises grow,
sweet smelling water lilies float
in dykes and ditches. Field edges
fill with colour, purple loose strife,
rose bay willow herb, ragged robin,
yellows of tansy and toadflax.
Up on Biggin Field are cowslips
and wild orchids.
Summer can bring drought,
once all was water,
then none.
Eels wriggle in pools
ditches dry up.
In isolated fens, there is
only ditch water to drink.
Now there is only mud.
An old woman crouches,
spooning muddy water into a kettle.

■ ■ ■

Fen Tigers work as farm labourers,
guide the horses up and down between
straight dykes to turn the light, dark soil,
which grows wheat, barley,
potatoes, celery, carrots.
A land not for grass growing,
too rich a resource.

At the Exhibition pub by the River Nene
bargees drink, talk of their journey
next day, when their pony will pull
their string of lighters up the Twenty Foot River,
through Priory Sluice to Upwell, Outwell and beyond.
Loads vary, bricks, potatoes, clunch, peat.
Along the road, the small Middle Level pub
has its usual crowd of field workers, puffing on clay pipes,
bowls turned down. In the front room
they stare at the bog oak fire and chunter
over the pub's history, always sold on
from Morgan's Brewery to Jenkins and Jones
and now to the landlord of the Red Cow.
It's livelier at the Ram on the Herne, more serious
at the Bucket and Spade in the shadow of the church.
Down Ramsey Heights the Golden Drop
and the True Briton are a riot of brickmakers
and small farmers calling for dates and Barceloney's.
By closing time at eleven, nut shells are wrecked
across the floor.

Fen Tigers run pumping mills, work small holdings,
they make a living and they pray.
Oh Lord how they pray.
Sunday is sacrosanct; scrub up,
best clothes for chapel, church and
Sunday school, hymn singing, gossip.
When they live too far out in the fens
the church comes to them.

The Reverend George Broke
gathers his flock two by two
into the Fenland Ark barge,
having sailed the gospel along
fen rivers to moor at four
isolated points for worship.
Fifty can crowd aboard
to raise their voices to God
accompanied by an organ.
Out in the windswept landscape
God seems very near.

Fen folk face water even in death,
not just by drowning but in the coffin.
Churchyard soil by the Old River Nene,
seeps water into newly dug graves
to claim its victim for a first, maybe a second time.
Dry weather brings no peace. The earth
cracks open and children, for a dare,
slide their hands down to touch the coffin.
A final indignity for the dead,
dry earth sinks and shifts makes new headstones
unstable. They lean, mimic
their companions, tilt and totter.

■ ■ ■

In winter, nineteen forty seven, temperatures plummet.
earth freezes down to the peat.
Snow fills dykes, drifts onto roads, doors, windows,
covers the Fens in a white shroud.

The thaw comes on the tenth of March,
rain too, more rain, snow melts,
soil remains frozen. Water, unable to seep away,
runs into rivers, levels rise and rise.

Across the Fens there is a scurry of activity.
Livestock are moved, potatoes riddled,
lorried away. Bags of clay to dam the cracks are rowed to
river banks or carried out on men's shoulders.

The abbey bell of Crowland tolls a warning.
There is a flood of biblical proportions.
The Great Ouse bank breaks near Ely, the river flows
over railway line and main road.

Men scramble in the dusk to damn disintegrating banks.
In a rising gale they lose the battle and themselves.
Water overwhelms, flattens houses, pours through buildings,
disintegrates barns.

Families sit on rooftops, lean out of first floor
windows, the view all water.
One farmer rows through the remains of his own home.
By March end two hundred thousand acres are flooded.

The rain stops. Huge pumps are brought from Holland.
They pump for weeks
and leave a muddy, oozy slud.
Soon the land is ploughed and planted.

Down by Raveley Drain on clear, windless nights
voices echo across Ramsey Heights, loud, peculiar,
"I have one." "Over here." "A rarity indeed."
"What they a'doin?" folk ask. Old Jackson's Fen,
wild now, once farmed, then dug for peat,
Rothschild bought it, uses it for walking
at night with flickering lights.
Men chasing moths.
There are reed beds, wet meadows, dragonflies,
butterflies, hen, marsh harriers,
sandpipers, redpolls, night heron
and the common crane
in Woodwalton Fen, a remnant place.

Night, no street or house lights in sight.
Twenty miles all round is our view, purple-blue
and a million stars. Tonight fireworks slit open
darkness. Rockets scorch up until a shower
of acid-green shines the sky clean.
A burst of rubies dim to Mars red.
Gold spangles dangle around Venus.
Catherine wheels and roman candles
conjure an aurora borealis at the horizon.
A final explosion fills the sky with ersatz stars
that plummet earthwards. Silence.
The originals reappear blinking,
holding fast to the firmament.

▪ ▪ ▪

What a view across the fields, twelve backsides in a row.
Nineteen twenty and women work in gangs. They crawl
over soft soil, up and down the rows to weed onions,
set potatoes, single sugar beet. To shield their faces
from the sun, bonnets are worn pulled tight, a frill
over the eyes, and one over the neck. One original
cuts a cardboard peak, twelve inches long, attaches
it to her bonnet. Soon all the gang have great beaks.
Like pecking birds they bow and nod to the black earth.
And peck they must in hard times, flood or cold
when food is scarce. "Jack Frost has frez the cupboard
doors to," they say as children fret.

Walk they must, to work, town, school,
five miles or more each way over cobbles or track,
short cuts across dykes on slippery, sagging planks.
In winter dark, children bunch tight in case
the Black Dog appears, harbinger of death.

These straight lines deceive, routes of danger,
B roads of sharp bends, wrong cambers, cracked tarmac,
surfaces slicked by rain, slimed by mud. Iced invisibility
skids early commuters into precipitate slides
down unfenced river banks, bonnets sucked down,
opaque water engulfs car roofs. Dripping metal carcasses
craned up out of the Forty Foot Drain or Old River Nene
with terrible regularity.

Wilting flowers mark bridge edges, tree trunks drape ribbons,
cards say "in Memory," "Why?" "Dear son."
Two hearses pass the cottage windows for two sons,
who met a tree before their time.
Lorries crash and thump along, cars accelerate.
These are ways to death.

At Easter young people walk the straight road,
carrying a large wooden cross. The procession
passes our three front windows,
a silent, unsettling vision.

Twenty thirty A.D.,
south of the Wash, below the siltlands, lie the Fens,
low-lying, water retaining windswept.
Sedges, reeds, wildfowl and fishes are its riches.
Wetland plants, purple moor grass,
one thousand species of moths, rare butterflies,
birds draw people here to wander
along footpaths, cycle paths and journey in boats.
Holme Fen wood, silver birch on peat to the North,
Woodwalton Fen to the South, water and fen between.
Three thousand seven hundred hectares of Nature Reserve,
the Black Fen.

▪ ▪ ▪

ACKNOWLEDGEMENTS

To Norma Pitfield I owe my sincere thanks for her support, encouragement and editorial skills on this poem.

To the Writer's Group and Café Poets who have listened to parts of the poem and offered their comments, many thanks.

Finally, very many thanks are due to Frances Osborn for bringing 'Black Fen' to pamphlet form.

SOURCES

I have read a large number of books about the area for the articles and the poem but three stand out for the very precise details they offer, Sybil Marshall's 'Fenland Chronicle', 'A Silver Knew Nothing' and 'A Pride of Tigers'.

‘Holme Wood’: painted by Christine Redington